Humility

THE EMPEROR'S NEW CLOTHES

Adapted by Mary Rowitz

Illustrated by Sherry Neidigh

Copyright © 2000 Publications International, Ltd.
ISBN: 0-7853-4312-1
Leap Frog is a trademark of Publications International, Ltd.

Once upon a time there was an emperor who loved clothes more than anything else. He had more clothes than anyone in the land. The emperor's clothes filled all the closets and most of the rooms in the royal palace.

It was a good thing the emperor was very rich, because he spent so much money on clothes. The emperor selected only the finest fabric, and he hired the best tailors to work for him.

The emperor also spent a lot of money on mirrors. He thought his fancy clothes made him look quite dashing, so he spent his free time looking at himself.

The emperor's pride was well-known throughout the kingdom. Everyone thought he was quite silly to spend so much time in front of his mirrors. They laughed at the emperor, but no one ever said anything directly to his face. They did not want to make the emperor angry because he was, after all, the ruler of the land.

Word of the silly emperor who loved fine clothes reached two thieves in a faraway land. Instead of making jokes about him, the thieves thought of a way that they could use the emperor's pride to make themselves rich.

The thieves dressed up as traveling tailors and made the long journey to the emperor's palace. They told the palace guards that they had the most wonderful fabric in all of the world, and they asked for permission to show it to the emperor. Of course, the guards let them into the palace.

The sneaky thieves presented themselves to the emperor and his wife. They explained that their fabric was not only wonderful, but magical, too. "Only the wisest people in the land will see this fabric," they said. "It will be invisible to fools and to those who are unfit for their office."

When the thieves opened their bags, the emperor squinted. He saw nothing at all in their hands! "Why, I must be a fool," thought the emperor. "Either that or I do not deserve to sit on this throne!" The emperor was embarrassed that he could not see the fabric, so he said, "That is the most magnificent fabric I have ever seen."

Then the emperor asked his wife what she thought of the magical fabric. She could not see anything, but she did not want anyone to think she was a fool, so she said, "It is quite extraordinary. It's like no other fabric that I know."

Knowing his wife was no fool, the emperor thought the fabric must be real, even though he could not see it. He offered the thieves twenty pieces of gold to make a new suit for him. They thanked the emperor and went to work right away.

"When you wear this suit, it will feel as light as a spider's web against your skin," one thief said as he measured the top of the emperor's head.

The other thief then explained, "You might even feel as though you're wearing nothing at all."

"I can't wait to try on my new suit," said the emperor excitedly. "It really sounds like it's the most wonderful fabric in the world!"

The thieves smiled slyly and winked at each other behind the emperor's back. They had finished sizing him up.

After a few days, the royal minister went to see how the new suit was coming along. He was going to tell the tailors to work as quickly as possible because the emperor was getting anxious and wanted to see his new suit as soon as possible.

The minister was stunned by what he did not see. The tailors were cutting away at the air with their scissors, and they were stitching up fabric that was not there! "Is it possible that I am a fool?" the minister gulped.

Seeing the minister, one of the thieves said, "Please tell the emperor that his suit will be ready soon. But first, please order another tray of food for us. All this hard work is making us very hungry."

Finally the thieves brought the emperor his new suit. He put it on slowly, being careful not to snag the fine stitching he could not see. Then he strutted around the room. He had never felt so dashing.

"This is the finest suit I have ever had," the emperor said to the royal minister. "What do you think of it?"

"If you are happy, then I am happy," said the royal minister, who was truly anything but happy. In his eyes, the emperor was standing in front of a mirror in his underwear, admiring a new suit that was not even there!

The emperor wanted to show off his new suit to everyone in the land. He asked the royal minister to call for a royal parade the next day.

Everyone in the kingdom was excited about the parade and the magical fabric. They had all heard that fools could not see the fabric, and they wanted to find out who among them was a fool and who was not.

On the day of the parade, everyone pushed and shoved to get the best view. But when the emperor appeared, everyone was shocked. The emperor was in his underwear!

Nobody wanted to look like a fool, so they said, "How handsome you look, Your Majesty. I never knew any fabric could look so wonderful."

Suddenly a young boy cried out over the noisy crowd. "The emperor isn't wearing a new suit!" he said. "What is everybody talking about? The emperor is wearing nothing but his underwear!"

Instantly the emperor knew that the boy was telling the truth. Everyone in the crowd began to laugh. They realized that they had all been foolish. They pretended to see a suit that was not even there. They felt silly for not telling the truth to the emperor.

After the parade, the embarrassed emperor quickly returned to the palace to put on some clothes. "Ah, that's better," the emperor said as he slipped on the robe. "I was beginning to get a chill from my magical suit." For the first time, the emperor left his room without looking in the mirror. Then he invited the honest young boy to speak with him in his court.

"I have decided to make you a junior minister. You have shown that you are very brave. You risked being called a fool to tell me the truth," the emperor said.

"Thank you," the boy said. "I will always be honest with you, even if you don't like what I have to say."

"I'm counting on it," said the emperor.

Humility

Humility means being humble or not proud. The emperor was so busy thinking about himself and his expensive clothes that he did not see that the thieves were lying to him. The emperor was too proud to admit that he could not see the invisible clothes. Then he was embarrassed in front of the whole kingdom!

The honest little boy made the emperor realize that true friends are more important than fancy clothes.